KEISHA'S MAZE MYSTERY

by Lauren Benson

Illustrations by
Dan Burr

Spot Illustrations by
Catherine Huerta

MagicAttic
Club

MAGIC ATTIC PRESS

Published by Magic Attic Press.

Copyright ©1997 by MAGIC ATTIC PRESS

For more information contact:
Book Editor, Magic Attic Press, 866 Spring Street,
P.O. Box 9722, Portland, ME 04104-5022

First Edition
Printed in the United States of America
2 3 4 5 6 7 8 9 10

Magic Attic Club is a registered trademark.

Betsy Gould, Publisher
Marva Martin, Art Director
Robin Haywood, Managing Editor

Edited by Laurie Orseck
Designed by Susi Oberhelman

ISBN 1-57513-090-4

Magic Attic Club books are printed on acid-free, recycled paper.

As members of the
MAGIC ATTIC CLUB,
we promise to
be best friends,
share all of our adventures in the attic,
use our imaginations,
have lots of fun together,
and remember—the real magic is in us.

Alison   *Keisha*

Heather   *Megan*

Table of Contents

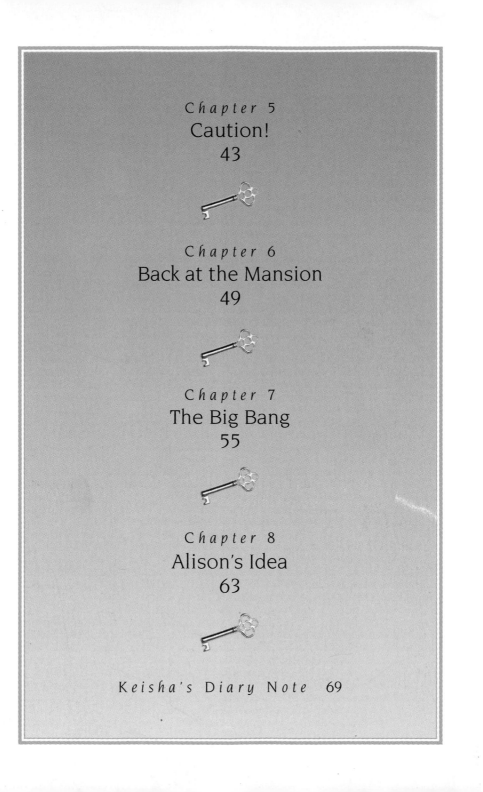

KEISHA'S
BAD MOOD

hat's the matter with Keisha?" Alison McCann whispered as she watched her friend stomp out of her house.

"I don't know," Heather Hardin whispered back. "But judging by the scowl on her face, she's in a bad mood."

"A really bad mood," Megan Ryder murmured.

Before the three girls could say anything more, Keisha Vance hurried down the front walk toward them. "Hi, you guys," she called. "Sorry I'm late. It's been a terrible morning."

"We can tell," Megan said sympathetically. "What's wrong?"

Keisha pushed back a strand of her long dark hair. "Well, first my alarm didn't go off, and I woke up late," she began. "And then Ronnie spilled syrup all over my new T shirt."

Alison rolled her eyes. "Little brothers can be such a pain in the neck," she said. "Last week my twin brothers used my report on ancient Egypt as ammunition in their paper airplane war!"

Alison was glad to see Keisha laugh despite her gloomy mood.

"I couldn't find my math book, which of course has my math homework in it," Keisha went on, "and then my dad gave me the worst news—Niki is coming to visit again."

"Niki?" Alison repeated. "As in Niki the Terrible?"

"You got it." Keisha grimaced. "And I'm dreading every minute of it."

"Who's Niki?" Heather asked as the four girls turned around and started walking toward school.

"My cousin from Ohio," Keisha explained. "She and her parents—Aunt Marion and Uncle Joseph—visit a few times every year."

Heather stopped to adjust her backpack. "So what's so terrible about her?" she asked.

"It's kind of hard to explain," Keisha admitted. "It's just that . . . well, last time Niki was here, all she wanted to do was hang around with Ronnie and Ashley. And when she wasn't playing with them, she was practicing her violin or performing a concert for my parents."

"That doesn't sound so terrible, Keisha," Heather pointed out.

"Trust me," Keisha retorted a little sharply. "Niki's not very friendly. She thinks she's really great just because she's a talented violinist."

"When is she coming?" Megan asked.

"Next Saturday," Keisha said, kicking a pebble and watching it bounce into the street. "Just in time to come to my mom's award dinner."

Keisha's mother was a nurse at the local hospital, and she'd recently received an award for her community service work. The dinner was being held at the fancy Brick Hotel downtown, and Keisha had been looking forward to getting dressed up and going with her family.

Soon the girls reached the corner near their school, Lincoln Elementary. As they stopped to wait for the traffic light to turn green, Heather glanced down at the sidewalk. Suddenly she noticed something.

"Uh, Keisha . . ." she started.

Keisha looked at her. "Yes?"

"Did you get dressed in the dark or something?" Heather went on, pointing downward.

Keisha looked down at her feet. On her right one she had on a black shoe with a silver buckle. On her left was one of her old brown loafers.

"Oh, no!" Keisha cried. She threw her hands into the air. "I don't believe this day!" Then she turned around and started running in the opposite direction. "I'll see you guys in a few minutes at school," she called over her shoulder. "I'm going home to change."

"Poor Keisha," Alison said as she stood with Heather and Megan on the sidewalk, watching Keisha race away. "Things really aren't going too well for her."

"And it sounds like they'll get worse next week when Niki comes," Megan said.

"Is Niki really that bad?" Heather asked as the girls started for school again.

Megan and Alison stopped and looked at each other.

"I didn't think so when I met her last summer," Megan confessed.

"I kind of liked her," Alison admitted. "I mean, she's quiet, but she struck me as pretty nice."

Heather shrugged. "Maybe Niki's visit will go better than Keisha thinks," she said hopefully.

"Mom?" Keisha called that afternoon as she entered her family's big sunny kitchen.

"I'm out here, baby," Mrs. Vance yelled from the backyard.

Keisha grabbed a few pretzels from a glass jar on the counter, then hurried outside. The warm spring sun was shining brightly, and a soft breeze stirred the trees. All around the yard, pale yellow daffodils and white tulips were in bloom. Keisha quickly spotted her mother, who was dressed in jeans, an old shirt, and a hat as she pulled weeds from one of the flower beds.

"Hey, Keisha girl," Mrs. Vance called warmly. "I'm glad you're home. How was your day?"

"Well, not so great, Mom," Keisha replied truthfully. She bit into her pretzel, then told her mother about everything from the alarm clock to her mismatched shoes.

Mrs. Vance shielded her eyes from the afternoon sun.

"Dad called me at work and said that you guys talked about it. Don't you want to baby-sit the younger kids with Niki?"

"Baby-sit?" Keisha repeated. "Dad didn't say anything about babysitting."

"He didn't?" Mrs. Vance said, looking surprised. "I know he had a hectic morning trying to get Ashley and Ronnie ready for day care. Maybe he didn't have time to mention it to you."

Keisha nodded. She folded her arms, waiting for her mother to go on.

Mrs. Vance stood up and took off her gardening gloves. "I could only get four tickets to the dinner," she said as she walked closer to Keisha, "so Dad and I thought that Aunt Marion and Uncle Joseph could come to the hotel with us while—"

Keisha finished her mother's sentence. "While I get stuck with Niki and baby-sitting the kids!"

"I know you were looking forward to going to the dinner, baby," Mrs. Vance replied. "But to tell you the truth, it'll probably be pretty boring. And Niki's your age," she reminded Keisha. "If you gave her a chance, I'm sure you'd find something in common."

"The last time she was here, she totally ignored me," Keisha reminded her mother. "All she wanted to do was play with Ashley and Ronnie and try to impress you and Dad with her stupid violin. I'm sorry, Mom, but I think Niki is a big show-off. She's—"

"That's quite enough, Keisha," Mrs. Vance cut in sharply. "Niki's a very nice girl who also happens to be your cousin," she said angrily, pulling her gloves back on. "You're spending next Saturday night with her and that's final!"

"Fine," Keisha shot back. Without another word, she spun around. I was wrong, she thought, flinging open the screen door. This isn't just a bad day. It's a *very* bad day!

Chapter

Two

A VISIT WITH ELLIE

re you sure your mom won't change her mind about you and Niki baby-sitting, Keisha?" Alison asked.

It was an hour later, and Keisha had called Alison to tell her about her conversation with her mother.

"Oh, I'm sure," Keisha grumbled. "Mom said her decision was final. That means I'm stuck at home next Saturday with Niki the Terrible."

Alison was quiet for a moment. "Maybe hanging out with Niki won't be so bad."

"That's easy for you to say," Keisha replied gloomily. "You're not the one who has to spend the whole weekend with her."

"Maybe we can think of a way to get you out of baby-sitting on Saturday night," Alison said. "Hey!" Her voice grew excited. "I have an idea. Maybe I can ask my mom if I can have a slumber party next weekend. She can call your mom and ask her if you can come."

"Thanks, Ali," Keisha said with a sigh. "That's really nice of you, but I know exactly what my mom's going to say: 'Sometimes family has to come first before friends.'"

"Oh well," Alison said, sounding disappointed. But then her voice perked up again. "As soon as we hang up, I'll call Megan and Heather. One of us is bound to think of something."

"Okay," Keisha said. "Sounds good." But when she hung up the phone a few minutes later, she didn't feel very optimistic. Somehow she knew that she'd be stuck at home with Niki, no matter what excuses her friends came up with.

Keisha opened the door to her room, where her younger sister and brother were playing.

"Vrooom! Vrooom!" Ronnie said, pushing a big red fire truck across the white and lavender rug.

"Hi, Keisha," five-year-old Ashley called. She was

sitting on Keisha's bed with a picture book in her lap. "Look at this picture of a Tyrannosaurus rex dinosaur. It's so cool."

"Mmmm," Keisha said. She barely glanced at the illustration.

Ashley looked up again. "Are you still in a bad mood, Keisha?" she asked, tugging on one of the ponytails at the top of her head.

Keisha nodded, surprised that her younger sister had noticed. "A little bit, Ashley," she admitted.

"Why are you so sad?" Ashley asked. She put down her book.

Keisha sighed. "Mom told me that I can't go to the award dinner with her and Dad. I have to stay home."

"To take care of me and Ronnie?" Ashley asked.

Keisha nodded. "Along with Niki," she added, making a face.

"Oh, goody!" Ashley exclaimed. "Niki is *so* nice. She's fun, too. I hope she brings her violin again."

"Well, I hope she leaves it at home!" Keisha snapped. First her dad and mom had told her how nice and talented Niki was, and now she was hearing it from Ashley, too. "I don't know why I even tried to talk to you about Niki," Keisha went on. "You're much too little to understand."

"No I'm not!" Ashley yelled. "You are!" Then she burst into tears and ran out of Keisha's room.

Ronnie had been watching the whole scene with his big brown eyes. "Is Niki going to play 'Twinkle, Twinkle, Little Star' on her violin?" he asked Keisha suddenly.

Keisha couldn't answer. Tears filled her eyes, and a lump formed in her throat.

"Bye, bye, Keisha," Ronnie mumbled, picking up his truck and scurrying out of the room.

As the door shut behind him, Keisha flung herself on the purple quilt that covered her bed.

Nice going, Keisha, she told herself. In about two seconds flat, she'd managed to hurt Ashley's feelings and drive poor Ronnie out of her room.

Keisha lay on her bed for a few minutes, feeling sorry for herself. Finally she stood up and hurried down the stairs.

"I'm going to Ellie Goodwin's house for awhile, Mom," she called. The screen door bounced once, then banged shut behind her.

"Would you like some lemonade, Keisha?" Ellie Goodwin asked.

"Okay," Keisha agreed.

She helped Ellie pour two tall glasses from a cobalt blue pitcher, then carried one over to the table in Ellie's cozy kitchen. The warm afternoon sunshine streamed in through a window as Keisha sat down in a chair painted a warm orange tone.

Ever since Ellie had moved into the white Victorian house on Primrose Lane, Keisha and her three best friends had spent many hours there. Every nook of Ellie's home seemed to contain something special. There were photographs of faraway places all over the walls, dozens of unusual musical instruments in her sitting room—she even owned a baseball autographed by Babe Ruth. But the four girls especially loved exploring the attic, where Ellie kept an old steamer trunk filled to the brim with interesting outfits. Whenever they tried on something from the trunk, they found themselves whisked off on an adventure in a new time and place.

"So what's wrong, dear?" Ellie asked as she joined Keisha at the table.

"How did you know something was wrong?" Keisha asked curiously.

Ellie was wearing a royal blue blouse that made her eyes look even more vibrant than usual. "Just a hunch," Ellie answered Keisha softly.

Keisha told Ellie about her day, ending with the fight she'd just had with Ashley. "I was pretty nasty," Keisha confessed. "I didn't mean to take out my anger on her—it just sort of happened."

"Hmmm," Ellie sipped her lemonade thoughtfully. "Well, it sounds like you're sorry, dear. I'm sure you can find a way to make it up to Ashley."

"That's true," Keisha said, thinking it over. "She loves

books—maybe I can offer to read her one tonight."

"That's a good start," Ellie said, nodding approvingly.

But that only solved half of Keisha's problems. "So what should I do about Niki?" she asked. "My mom and dad keep saying that I have to give her another chance. But I don't want to. She's not very friendly, and she never tries to get to know me better." She sipped her lemonade. "Maybe Alison *will* think of a way to get me out of spending Saturday night with Niki."

"Knowing Alison," Ellie said, a twinkle in her blue eyes, "she probably will." Her expression turned more serious. "You know, Keisha, sometimes we all have to do things that we don't want to do. In fact," she went on, glancing at the clock, "I'm doing a favor for a friend in a few minutes."

"You are?" Keisha said.

Ellie nodded. "My friend asked me to give voice lessons to her husband. He retired from his job recently, and he's trying to find some new interests. But I have to confess I've been dreading the lesson all day."

"Why?" Keisha asked curiously. Ellie taught drama and music lessons in her home, and Keisha had always thought that she enjoyed it very much.

"I have plenty of students right now," Ellie explained, "and I don't really have time to take on someone new.

Besides that," she went on, smiling a little, "I spoke to Mr. O'Brien on the phone, and I got the feeling that he can barely carry a tune."

"Oh," Keisha said. She couldn't help smiling at the thought of Ellie trying to give voice lessons to a man who sang off-key.

Just then, the doorbell rang.

"There he is," Keisha said. "Good luck, Ellie," she added, still smiling.

"Thank you," Ellie said. As she stood up, she made a suggestion. "Why don't you head upstairs to the attic for awhile? I bet it'll do you a world of good."

"That's a great idea," Keisha agreed. She hurried over to the sink with her empty glass. A trip to the attic would definitely cheer her up.

Chapter
Three

THE GARDEN PARTY

eisha turned the key in the lock and pushed open the door leading to the attic. Outside dusk had fallen, and the streetlamps along the curb were on, filling the room with a soft yellow glow.

Keisha pulled the satin cord on the overhead light, then glanced at the old steamer trunk. It sat in its usual place, almost as if it were waiting for her. She tiptoed over to it, eager to see what she would find inside.

Keisha lifted the heavy lid and began to sort through a

pile of clothes. She set aside a pair of silky pink harem pants and a gymnast's leotard that glittered with sequins. Then she noticed a colorful dress made of a bright floral fabric. With its soft shades of pink and lavender and green, it made her think of summer and a garden in full bloom. It had a wide satin sash and a white collar trimmed in lace. Next to the dress lay a pair of white tights and matching shoes.

As she held the dress in her fingers, Keisha couldn't help thinking about next weekend again. She had hoped she'd be getting dressed up in an outfit like this one to go to the award dinner at the Brick Hotel.

Suddenly Keisha's mind was made up. She carefully slipped on the dress, tights, and shoes, then put the other things back in the trunk. As she turned toward the tall, gilt-edged mirror, she spotted something on the hat rack. It was a wide-brimmed white straw hat encircled by a lavendar satin ribbon and sprinkled with flowers. It would look perfect with her dress.

Keisha put the hat on, and sat on the edge of the trunk and stared back into the mirror.

I look like I'm ready for a party, she thought happily. An elegant party with . . .

Suddenly the soft lighting of Ellie's attic faded away.

Keisha heard a murmur of voices and the clinking of

glasses before she realized that she was standing outside in the bright afternoon sun. A waiter carrying a gleaming silver tray filled with delicious-looking pastries brushed past her.

I *am* at a party, Keisha thought as she looked around. A garden party!

Keisha blinked hard, trying to get used to the bright sunshine. Set back from the lush green lawn was a beautiful Tudor-style mansion. Several women stood in the grass nearby, their light summer dresses fluttering in the breeze. The soft pastel shades of their outfits made her think of lemon and lime sherbet.

"Keisha?"

Keisha whirled around to see who'd spoken her name. A girl who looked about her age was coming toward her. Her long dark hair was pulled away from her face and tied with a wide satin ribbon. She had warm, friendly brown eyes.

"It's your turn, silly," the girl said, thrusting a croquet mallet into Keisha's hand. "Were you daydreaming or something?"

"Sorry about that," Keisha mumbled. She'd been so distracted by the mansion and the people standing on the lawn, she hadn't noticed the croquet balls and hoop-shaped wickets set up near her feet.

Keisha quickly swung at a purple ball near her feet— and missed by a good six inches.

"Nice shot, Keisha!" a boy said, laughing loudly. "Amanda and I shouldn't have too much trouble beating *you*."

"Oh, be quiet, Blair," the girl named Amanda scolded him. "Try again, Keisha," she said. "That shot doesn't count, okay?"

"Okay." Keisha felt her face flush as she gripped the mallet again. This time she tried to concentrate before she swung. *Smack*! She neatly knocked her ball through one of the white wickets.

"Not bad," Blair called.

"Thanks." Keisha looked up and flashed him a smile. Blair had black curly hair and a good-natured grin. He wore baggy khaki shorts and a T shirt that was printed with a fake tie and lapels.

As the three of them continued playing croquet, Keisha looked around to try to learn more about where she was. So far all she knew was that she had arrived at a party on the grounds of a beautiful estate. But as Amanda and Blair continued talking back and forth, Keisha figured out that the party was being held for the students at their school, Pennington Academy, to celebrate the end of the school year.

Keisha stepped up to her ball to take another turn. Just then she noticed a white-haired man with a cane slowly making his way across the green lawn toward them. "Having fun, everyone?" he called.

"You bet, Mr. Crawford," Blair called back. "Longwood Estate is such a cool place to have a party."

"Thank you, Blair," Mr. Crawford said, beaming. "The students from Pennington do seem to have a good time here every year. I've been hosting a summer party for them for over sixty years." He shook his head. "Can you youngsters believe that?"

"Wow," Keisha said, amazed. "That's a long time. Your estate is really beautiful, Mr. Crawford," she went on. "I've never seen such pretty flowers."

Mr. Crawford nodded. "I think Longwood is one of the loveliest places on earth," he said. "Sometimes it makes me quite sad to think . . . " Suddenly, his eyes clouded over and his words trailed off. For a moment, the elderly gentleman just stared off into space, as if he was lost in thought. Then he seemed to snap back to attention. "Oh, never mind. Carry on, you three," he went on. "And make sure you explore the maze before the day's over. Everyone loves to have an adventure in there." He chuckled before moving away to chat with another group of guests.

A garden maze? Keisha felt a tingle of excitement. One of her favorite books was *The Secret Garden*, a story about a girl who discovers a whole new world behind a walled garden. Keisha would love to have the chance to explore one. "Is there really a maze on the grounds?" she asked Amanda.

Amanda nodded. "It's over there," she said, pointing to the row of tall hedges in the distance beyond the fish pond. "It's a really big and elaborate one. My friend Sarah and I explored it at Mr. Crawford's party last year. We got lost about five times before we found our way out!"

"It sounds great," Keisha said wistfully.

"We can check it out after we're finished playing croquet," Amanda said as she swung her mallet.

"It might be your last chance to see the maze, you know," Blair chimed in suddenly.

"What do you mean?" Keisha asked.

"Mr. Crawford is pretty old," Blair explained. "And my mom told me that he's thinking of giving Longwood away before he dies."

"What about his family?" Keisha asked. "Don't they want to live here?"

Blair shrugged. "I'm not sure. All I know is that there are rumors around that he might donate it to a museum."

"That's not what I heard," an unfamiliar voice said.

Keisha turned. A girl a few years older than Keisha was standing with a group of her friends. She was wearing a pale pink dress and a matching hat.

"What did you hear, Monica?" Blair asked.

"My aunt told me that Mr. Crawford doesn't want to give the estate away. His son, David, is pressuring him into selling it to a developer who wants to build houses and a big shopping center here."

"Oh, no." Amanda looked upset. "But the estate is so beautiful. He can't sell it to someone who wants to turn it into a shopping center!"

"His son might make him," Monica said in a low voice. She looked around to make sure no one else was close by. "The family could get millions of dollars for Longwood Estate, you know." Then she flipped her long blond hair over her shoulder and wandered off toward the tennis courts with her friends.

"What terrible news," Amanda said.

"It's only a rumor," Blair reminded her. "And you know Monica—she's the biggest gossip at Pennington."

As the other two kids talked, Keisha gazed around the lush grounds. Everywhere she looked she saw flower beds overflowing with bright, colorful blossoms. Tall stands of pink daylilies surrounded the fish pond, and nearby a fountain was gently spurting clear, cool water. In the distance were two clay tennis courts and a sparkling blue swimming pool. Keisha couldn't imagine how anyone could even consider selling a place as beautiful as Longwood—especially to a builder who wanted to destroy it.

No wonder Mr. Crawford looked a little sad earlier, Keisha thought. He was probably upset at the idea of selling the estate.

Just then Blair swung his mallet hard, sending his ball soaring into the sky.

"I'll get it!" Keisha yelled. She kept her eye on the ball as it bounced down onto a hill, gaining speed as it rolled past the fish pond and approached the maze.

As Keisha chased after the runaway ball, she noticed a man several yards ahead of her, hurrying toward the maze as well. He glanced nervously over his shoulder a few times, as if he were checking to see if anyone was following him.

That man doesn't look like a guest at the party, Keisha thought, noticing his worn brown jacket and the satchel in his hand. As he ducked inside the maze, she wondered if he was a caretaker or gardener.

The ball finally came to a stop near the entrance to the maze. Keisha ran over and picked it up. As her fingers closed around it, she heard hushed voices on the other side of the tall hedges.

"Did you get everything?" a man with a deep voice demanded.

"I sure did," another man replied. "We're all set for eight o'clock tonight."

"Good." A chill went through Keisha as the first man started laughing. "This party is going to end with a bang," he said. "A really big bang."

chapter Four

INSIDE
THE MAZE

shiver raced up Keisha's spine. As the two voices seemed to move deeper inside the maze, she stood completely still. She couldn't believe what she had just heard.

"Keisha!" Blair yelled suddenly, startling her. He and Amanda appeared at the top of the hill. "What's taking you so long?"

"Did you find the ball, Keisha?" Amanda called.

Keisha quickly scooped up the blue ball and held it up

for her friends to see. Then she hurried back up the hill and told them about the two men. "I think we'd better do something," she said worriedly. "What if they're planning something dangerous?"

"Come on, Keisha. You've been reading too many mysteries," Blair said, laughing.

"You didn't hear these guys talking about a big bang," Keisha insisted. "They sounded serious."

"A big bang?" Blair pretended to look worried. "Maybe that guy was hiding a dangerous weapon in his satchel!"

"Oh, stop teasing Keisha," Amanda chided Blair. But Keisha could tell from the expression on Amanda's face that she wasn't taking this very seriously, either.

"Suppose those two guys are planning something dangerous, Keisha," Amanda said. "What can we do about it?"

Keisha glanced over her shoulder at the maze. "I want to follow them," she said. "Maybe we can find out what they're up to.

"Boy, you do think you're Sherlock Holmes, don't you?" Blair was still making fun of her. "Want me to go ask Mr. Crawford for a

magnifying glass so you can search the maze for clues?"

Amanda grinned, but Keisha was too worried to laugh.

"Come on, Keisha," Amanda coaxed her. "Forget about it. Those guys are probably gardeners or maintenance men or something."

"Right," Blair added. "Let's just finish the game," he said, turning around and heading back to where they'd been playing croquet.

Amanda started to follow, but Keisha hung back. She couldn't shake the feeling that something terrible was going to happen at the party that evening.

Amanda stopped and looked at her. "Aren't you coming?" she called.

Keisha shook her head. "You guys don't have to come with me, but I'm going into the maze."

"You can't go by yourself," Amanda reminded her. "It's too easy to get lost."

"So come with me," Keisha said, waving her over. "Even if we don't find those guys, you can show me the maze."

Amanda hesitated for just a second. "Oh, all right," she finally agreed. She yelled good-bye to Blair before hurrying down the hill. "I still think you're worrying about nothing, but I can't let you go alone." Amanda rolled her eyes and grinned. "I just hope you realize that we'll never hear the end of this from Blair."

"We'll see about that," Keisha said. "If we find out that something's really going on, Blair's going to wish that he had come with us."

A moment later, the two girls rounded the hedges and entered the maze.

"This is incredible," Keisha murmured as she stepped inside. It felt as if she'd entered a whole new world. The hedges were as tall as the walls of a room, blocking off the girls' view of the rest of the estate. Several gravel-lined paths led off in different directions. From where they stood, they could see beds of flowers and blooming shrubs and dense ground cover. Scattered about the gardens were sculpted statues, many of winged cherubs or figures that reminded Keisha of Greek gods and goddesses. The late-afternoon sun blazed overhead, but in the maze it felt cool and shady.

Keisha looked at the pathways, then glanced back at Amanda. "Which way?" she asked.

Amanda shrugged. "Your guess is as good as mine."

Keisha finally chose a path off to the right. She and Amanda followed the walkway past several small reflecting pools and a sea of yellow black-eyed Susans and tall white daisies.

After ten minutes of following the path, Keisha glanced nervously behind her. The maze was huge, with

hundreds of twists and turns. So far they hadn't seen a trace of the men—what if they never found them? Even worse, what if she and Amanda never found their way back out?

Stop it! Keisha chided herself. She couldn't let herself think spooky thoughts. She and Amanda could wander through the maze for awhile longer, she decided, then easily find their way back if they didn't find the men.

The girls made several more turns before the path led under a row of wooden archways. English ivy grew thickly over the top, blocking out the sunlight.

"This is pretty neat," Amanda said.

Keisha nodded. She felt as if she'd entered a long tunnel.

"Ssshhh." Amanda whispered suddenly. She waved for Keisha to be quiet.

"I'm telling you," a man's deep voice was saying, "he doesn't have a clue about what's coming."

"It's them!" Keisha whispered.

"It'll be quite a shock," the man continued. "He's eighty-five today, you know. I hope his heart holds out for my . . . uh . . . little surprise."

Amanda's eyes went wide.

"Don't worry," the other man replied. "Everything will go off just as we planned. In my line of work, I can't afford to make mistakes."

"I'm sure," the first man said. "It's way too dangerous."

The second man said something back, but Amanda was gripping Keisha's arm so tightly that she couldn't concentrate.

"What is it?" Keisha hissed at Amanda.

"I recognize the first man's voice!" Amanda whispered excitedly. "I know who that is!"

"You do?" Keisha said.

Amanda nodded. "It's David—Mr. Crawford's son!"

"Really?" Keisha blinked in surprise. "Are you sure?"

Amanda nodded, then held a finger over her lips. The girls tried to listen again, but the men's voices had drifted farther away.

Keisha turned back to Amanda. "Why would Mr. Crawford's son be planning to end the party 'with a big bang'?"

"I don't know," Amanda said, shaking her head.

The girls fell silent for a few minutes, lost in thought. Then something occurred to Keisha. "Maybe whatever's going on has something to do with all the rumors about Mr. Crawford's selling Longwood Estate. Maybe Mr. Crawford doesn't want to sell and David's doing something to make him! Have you ever met David?"

"Lots of times at Pennington Academy," Amanda

replied. "He seems pretty nice."

"Well, whatever he's planning doesn't sound nice," Keisha said. "It sounds pretty scary." She grabbed Amanda's arm. "Come on. Let's keep following them. Maybe we can find out more about what they're planning to do."

"Okay," Amanda agreed. "But then I think we should turn back and tell Mr. Crawford or one of the teachers at the party."

Keisha nodded, then led the way along the gravel path. As the girls walked, long shadows spilled over them. Keisha didn't want to say anything to Amanda, but she knew it would be dark in another hour or so. Then it would really be impossible to navigate through the maze.

Twice Keisha made a wrong turn that led them to a dead end. As they turned around the second time and started in the opposite direction, a loud noise filled the air.

"What was that?" Keisha gasped, whirling around to face Amanda.

Amanda bit her lip. "I don't know," she said, nervously looking around.

Screeech!

Keisha jumped as the horrible noise came again. The girls froze in their tracks, scanning the shrubs and flowers around them. Just then Keisha heard a rustling sound behind a clump of bushes with bright pink blossoms. Her heart pounded as the bushes rustled again.

Screeech!

With a furious squawk, something suddenly burst out from behind the shrubs.

Keisha opened her mouth to scream—until she saw what stood in front of them.

Amanda laughed. "It's a peacock!" She exclaimed.

Keisha stared in amazement at the large bird just a few feet away on the path, its long colorful feathers spread out behind him like a fan.

"He looks as surprised to see us as we are to see him," Keisha said.

As the peacock dropped his feathers and strutted off toward another part of the maze, the girls smiled and continued on their way. Keisha listened carefully, hoping to hear the men's voices. But the only sound was an occasional yelp from the peacock or a squawk from the black crows hovering above the trees in the distance.

A short while later, Keisha stopped near a cluster of shrubs arranged to form a circle. In the center of the neatly trimmed hedges was a fountain surrounded by flowers.

"I hate to admit it," Keisha sighed, "but I'm beginning to think that following those guys is hopeless. We're never going to find them."

"It's been awhile since we heard them talking," Amanda agreed. She looked up at the sky. The sun had dropped below the hedges. Keisha knew that Amanda was now thinking exactly   as she was: In another hour it would be dark. Then it would be almost impossible to find their way out.

Keisha glanced around, trying to locate an exit or figure out how to get back to where they'd entered the maze.

Suddenly, her eye caught a flash of brown about thirty feet away, near the statue of a graceful-looking Greek goddess. It took a few seconds for Keisha's brain to register what her eyes were seeing: A man in a brown coat was disappearing into a large hole in the ground!

Chapter
Five

CAUTION!

hocked, Keisha elbowed Amanda. "There he is!" she whispered. "There's the man I saw going into the maze!" She couldn't believe what she was seeing—it was like a scene from *Alice's Adventures in Wonderland*.

"Where does that hole lead?" Amanda whispered.

"I don't know," Keisha answered grimly, "but I'm going to find out."

Keisha cautiously started toward the hole, with Amanda close on her heels. As she drew nearer, she noticed a large stone plaque resting in the grass next to the hole. To Keisha's astonishment, it was slowly shifting. A second later, it had completely covered the opening in the ground!

"Omigosh," Amanda whispered. "I've really got the creeps now."

Keisha tried to ignore the uneasy feeling settling in her bones as she bent down and looked at the plaque more closely. It was made of white stone and in the center was an inscription: A *garden quenches the soul's deepest thirst*.

Tentatively, Keisha reached out and pushed on the stone. It didn't budge. She tried again, this time using more force. Still it didn't move.

Amanda tried to move the plaque a few times, too. Finally, she gave up and leaned back against the tall statue. "Come on, Keisha," she said. "Let's just get out of here. We can find one of the teachers and—"

Just then the stone suddenly began to shift again.

"It's the statue!" Keisha cried, looking at Amanda. "That statue must somehow make the stone move!"

"No way," Amanda said. But as she pushed against the statue again, the plaque slid away from the opening once more.

Keisha knelt and peered down into the hole. Roughly cut steps led down into what looked like a long tunnel.

"Come on," she said to her friend. "Let's see what's down there." Before Amanda could reply, Keisha started down the stairs.

"I don't know about this," Amanda murmured as she reluctantly followed. "It looks pretty creepy down here."

"Don't worry," Keisha said, trying to sound calm. "We're just going to see where this leads, and then I promise we're out of here."

But as they descended into the darkness, the air turned chilly and damp, and Keisha felt her stomach tighten. It's really dark down here, she thought. And it could be dangerous, too. She had no idea what Mr. Crawford's son and his friend were up to—or what they would do if they discovered that someone was following them.

Keisha forced herself to continue on through the dark tunnel. As the girls rounded a bend, Keisha was relieved to see lit torches mounted along the wall. At least now they could see where they were going.

Suddenly, Keisha felt a sharp tug on the sash of her dress.

"Did you hear something?" Amanda whispered.

"No." Keisha listened carefully.

Thud! Thud!

This time she heard several loud noises, followed by shuffling sounds, as if someone were moving something around. Then she heard voices murmuring back and forth.

She and Amanda exchanged frightened looks.

A moment later, the shuffling stopped, then footsteps faintly echoed through the tunnel.

Keisha stiffened, expecting the footsteps to come closer. Instead they grew fainter, as if the men were headed in the opposite direction.

Keisha motioned for Amanda to follow her as she grabbed one of the torches. Thoughts flooded her mind as she led the way through the passageway. What if the man's satchel really did contain weapons? What if the two men really were dangerous? She and Amanda were trapped in the maze without the slightest idea how to get out.

Keisha's heart was pounding by the time the tunnel widened into a larger room.

"This looks like a storage area," Keisha said. She began to look around more carefully. In the torches' flickering lights, she could see cobwebs clinging to the corners of the small chamber, as well as several empty plastic bottles and an old newspaper strewn about on the ground.

"Omigosh!" Keisha gasped and jumped back as a big black spider skittered along the dirt floor near her feet.

But Amanda hadn't noticed the creepy spider. She was staring at the wall, where several rows of crates were stacked up. "Look at this stuff," she murmured. "I wonder what's in the boxes."

Trying to make out the bold letters printed on the boxes, Keisha held the lit torch near one of the boxes. An ominous warning jumped out at her:

**CAUTION! EXPLOSIVE MATERIAL.
HIGHLY FLAMMABLE!**

Chapter

Six

BACK AT THE
MANSION

xplosives!" Amanda gasped when she saw the
warning printed on the box. "Quick, Keisha! Get rid
of that torch!"

For a second, Keisha's heart seemed to stop beating.
The lit torch in her hand could make the explosives blow
up, she realized. In a panic, she lunged across the room
and quickly put it back in its spot along the wall.

This time, when Amanda grabbed her arm and said,
"Let's go," Keisha wasn't about to argue.

Down the long stretch of tunnel off to the right, Keisha noticed another staircase. "This way," she instructed Amanda. The girls dashed toward the steps and raced up them. Keisha's mind was spinning. David Crawford must be planning to blow up his father's estate she decided. There was no other explanation.

The long staircase led into the open air near a bed of purple flowers and several dogwood trees. Looking around, Keisha saw that they were out of the maze, in an unfamiliar part of the gardens.

"What time is it?" Keisha asked Amanda, panting.

"Probably around seven or seven-thirty," Amanda replied, glancing around at the twilight. "Why?"

"I think David Crawford's planning to blow up the estate," Keisha told her. "And I think he's going to do it at eight o'clock tonight."

Amanda gasped. "We have to find Mr. Crawford and tell him what's going on!"

Over the top of the trees, Keisha spotted several tall chimneys. "There's the mansion!"

The two girls tore past the flower beds and trees and quickly reached the rolling lawn behind the mansion.

As they drew closer to the house, Amanda had an idea. "I remember seeing a gatehouse when we came up the driveway. I'll head there to tell the security guards about the explosives. You head up to the house and get Mr. Crawford, okay?"

"Okay," Keisha agreed. Amanda took off for the driveway while Keisha raced toward the backyard, holding onto her straw hat so she wouldn't lose it.

About a dozen people were sitting around on the lawn furniture talking while a bunch of kids played tag. Keisha looked around nervously, wondering where David Crawford was. But right now she had to find his father.

"Has anyone seen Mr. Crawford?" she called out.

A man in a blue suit lowered his glass. "I believe Mr. Crawford is in his study having tea with several of the guests."

"Thank you," Keisha yelled as she headed for the double French doors that led inside the mansion.

Keisha entered a beautifully decorated sitting room. When she reached the hallway beyond, she came to a halt. This house was huge—how in the world was she ever going to figure out where the study was?

Just then she noticed a man pushing a tea cart filled with pastries, a polished teapot, and several delicate-looking china teacups. He must be going to the study, Keisha guessed. She hurried after him as he turned into a large room with dark paneling and tall bookshelves. The windows were open and white curtains billowed in the soft evening breeze as six or seven people stood together talking and sipping tea.

Keisha frantically looked around until she saw Mr. Crawford seated in a wide leather chair. His back was to her as he chatted with a young man in a dark suit.

For a second, Keisha stood frozen, uncertain what to do. She didn't want to interrupt Mr. Crawford, but this was an emergency!

As Keisha stood there, hesitating, the young man suddenly noticed her. As he approached, Keisha could see that his hair was wet, as if he'd just showered, and he was straightening his tie.

He stopped in front of Keisha and held out a hand. "Hello," he said warmly. "I don't believe we've met."

Oh, no, Keisha thought impatiently, I can't talk to this man now. But she quickly introduced herself. It was ten to eight according to the clock over the fireplace. She had to get Mr. Crawford's attention right away.

"Welcome to Longwood, Keisha," the young man was saying. "I make it a point to meet all the students at Pennington. My father is devoted to the school, as you

can tell, and he absolutely loves hosting the end-of-the-year party every spring."

Keisha tuned out as the man went on. Suddenly something clicked in her brain—the man's deep voice was so familiar. And she knew exactly where she'd heard it before—inside the maze!

"You're David Crawford," she blurted out.

Chapter
Seven

THE BIG BANG

hy, yes, of course, I'm David Crawford," the man
said, looking surprised at Keisha's reaction. "I
know I'm late for the party," he went on in a low voice, "but
I've been very busy planning a big surprise for my dad."

Keisha stared at him, shocked that he'd even reveal
that much to her. "I know what you're planning," she said
coldly. "And I—"

"You know what I'm planning?" David interrupted her.

Keisha nodded, gathering courage as she spoke."My

friend Amanda and I followed you this afternoon, and we saw your supplies in the maze."

"Dad doesn't know, does he?" David asked in a worried tone.

"Not yet," Keisha said. "But I was just about to tell him."

David gripped her arm. "Oh, please don't, Keisha," he said. "Dad didn't want to make a big fuss, but today's his birthday. I planned the fireworks as a surprise."

Suddenly Keisha felt as if a cold bucket of water had been dumped over her head.

"Fireworks?" she repeated. Her whole body went numb. "Did you say you were planning a fireworks display for your father?"

"Yes." David nodded. Then he looked at her quizzically. "What did you think I was planning?"

"Oh no," Keisha mumbled. "I don't believe this."

"Keisha? Are you okay?" David asked, sounding concerned.

"No," Keisha said woodenly. "I'm not." She forced herself to look David in the eye. "I made a terrible mistake," she finally said.

"What do you mean?" David looked totally confused. "What kind of mistake? Surely it's not as terrible as you think it is."

"Oh, yes it is," Keisha replied. She took a deep breath,

then told him the whole story—how she had heard him talking in the maze and followed him to the secret underground room, where she had seen the explosives.

David seemed more shocked than angry. "You really believed that I was going to blow up my father's estate?" he asked.

"I thought you were trying to make him sell it or something," Keisha said. A fresh wave of embarrassment washed over her. How could she have believed something so crazy?

"Actually, I don't know why I'm so surprised," David said with a sigh. "There are so many rumors about my family's estate floating around. It's a good thing that Dad's planning to make his big announcement tonight. It'll end those stories once and for all."

"What big announcement?" Keisha asked.

David hesitated, then smiled faintly. "I probably shouldn't tell you this, but somehow the circumstances seem to call for it," he said, lowering his voice. "Dad's donating the estate to Pennington Academy."

"What?" Keisha exclaimed in an excited whisper. "He's donating the estate to the school—what a relief!"

Just then David glanced at his watch. He turned toward the guests in the room. "Come on, everyone," he called out. "There's a big surprise out on the back lawn!"

As everyone started murmuring and following David out the door, Keisha couldn't wait to tell Blair and Amanda that—

"Oh no!" Keisha cried, suddenly slapping a hand over her mouth. She had been so distracted by her conversation with David Crawford that she'd completely forgotten that Amanda had gone to tell the security guards about the explosives!

Keisha whirled around and shot toward the door. She had to find Amanda right away!

Keisha flung open the double French doors that opened onto the backyard. It was dark outside now, except for some floodlights scattered around the grounds and fireflies flickering across the broad, rolling lawn. Everyone was chattering excitedly about the "big surprise" that David had planned. Keisha quickly scanned the grounds, but she didn't see Amanda or the security guards anywhere.

As she ran to the front of the house, Keisha spotted Amanda

hurrying up the long driveway. Behind her were two guards in blue uniforms, flashlights in hand.

"Amanda!" Keisha yelled. She waved desperately to her friend. "We made a big mistake!"

Keisha could see a confused expression on Amanda's face as she drew closer. "What do you mean we made a mistake, Keisha? I just told the guards about the explosives in the tunnel."

The taller guard nodded. "That's right, miss. Explosives are a dangerous business. Have you alerted Mr. Crawford?"

"Yes . . . no . . . well . . ." Keisha stuttered for a second before the story tumbled out.

"Oh no!" Amanda exclaimed. "I'm so embarrassed."

"It's not your fault, Amanda," Keisha tried to reassure her. "I'm the one who just assumed that David was planning to blow up Longwood Estate."

The guard shook his head. "No harm done this time, girls. But it sounds like you jumped to conclusions before you had all the facts."

Keisha nodded ruefully. She had definitely learned a lesson. But before she could say as much to the guards, she heard a loud noise.

"Oh, look!" Amanda cried. "The fireworks have started."

Keisha glanced up as brilliant pink, green, and white lights burst against the black sky.

The girls thanked the guards, then ran to the backyard, where the rest of the guests had gathered to watch the display.

"Oooooh," everyone murmured as blue, green, and yellow lights exploded overhead. "Aaaaahhhh."

As she watched the display, Keisha glanced over at the patio, where the elder Mr. Crawford was standing arm-in-arm with his son, his eyes fixed on lights and colors raining down over them. From where she stood on the damp grass, Keisha could see that the older man looked tired, but he was smiling contentedly.

Happy Birthday, Mr. Crawford, Keisha wished him silently. Even though she wouldn't be there later to hear his important announcement, she knew that all the guests would greet the news with a big cheer. His beautiful gardens and the rest of the estate would be enjoyed by the Pennington students for a long time into the future.

Keisha waited until the last of the fireworks went off, then quietly slipped away from the crowd. She found a powder room on the first floor and looked into the mirror.

A moment later she was back in Ellie's attic.

Chapter
Eight

ALISON'S IDEA

s Keisha folded the flowered dress and carefully placed it inside the trunk, a man's deep, melodious voice drifted up through the attic floorboards. She paused for a second, listening to the beautiful hymn he was singing, which she recognized right away from choir practice.

"All things bright and beauteous. All creatures great and small . . ."

At first Keisha thought the music was coming from

Ellie's stereo, but
then it dawned on
her: The man who
was singing was Mr.
O'Brien, Ellie's new student.

Ellie was completely wrong, Keisha thought. Mr.
O'Brien wasn't a terrible singer—he had a wonderful rich
baritone voice.

A smile slowly crept across Keisha's face. Somehow it
felt good to know that she wasn't the only one who had
jumped to conclusions.

Keisha closed the trunk and tiptoed down the stairs,
being careful not to disturb Ellie and her pupil. As she
crossed the street to her house, she found herself softly
singing the words to the familiar hymn. By the time she
pushed open the back door to her house, she realized that
her bad mood had completely disappeared.

Keisha's parents were sitting at the kitchen table,
chopping vegetables for a salad for dinner. As soon as she
walked into the room, Keisha could tell that the two of
them were discussing something important.

"Hey, Keisha," Mr. Vance called. "Mom and I were just
talking about you."

"You were?" Keisha said nervously. They'd probably
been talking about how cranky she'd acted all day.

Mrs. Vance nodded and patted the chair next to her. "Dad and I decided that we didn't handle things very well. We're not going to make you stay home next weekend and baby-sit with Niki."

"You're not?" This was the last thing Keisha had expected her parents to say.

"Nope," her dad said. "Now that we've had a chance to think about it, we realize we didn't think our plans through very well—and we didn't take into account how much you were counting on attending the dinner. You still have to be nice to Niki while she's visiting," Mr. Vance continued with a smile, "but if you want to come to the award dinner with us, we'll find a way to get another ticket for the family."

"And a way for you to get a new dress to wear," Mrs. Vance chimed in.

"Thanks, you guys," Keisha said, smiling back at her parents. For a minute she didn't say anything more as she tried to sort out her feelings. She hadn't thought about Niki's visit since her trip to the attic, and now, to her surprise, she felt differently about seeing her cousin. "You know what?" she said suddenly. "I don't really mind staying home with the younger kids and Niki after all."

"You don't?" Mrs. Vance said. She stopped slicing a cucumber and gave Keisha a surprised look.

"No." Keisha shook her head. "No offense, Mom, but the

dinner will probably be a little boring, and it doesn't seem fair to leave her home alone with the little kids."

"Are you sure?" her father asked. "We'd love to have you come."

Keisha shook her head. "I'm positive, Dad."

"Well, I'm very proud of you," her mother said, giving Keisha a quick hug. "I know you hate it when I say this," she added, grinning, "but I think you just made a very mature decision."

Keisha was about to find Ashley and apologize when the doorbell rang.

"I'll get it!" Ashley said, racing out of the family room. "Keisha! Your friends are here!"

Keisha hurried to the front door where Alison, Heather, and Megan were standing under the porch light.

"Hey, Keisha," Alison said even before Keisha reached the door. "I know it's almost dinnertime, but we had to come over. I have a great idea to get you out of baby-sitting next weekend."

"Actually, Alison, I—" Keisha started. But Alison was talking so rapidly that Keisha couldn't get a word in edgewise.

"You can tell your parents that you absolutely have to come over next Saturday and spend all day and night with me or you'll never see me again."

"It's true," Heather chimed in.

Keisha burst out laughing. "Ali, you're the best," she said. "You, too, Megan and Heather," she added, holding open the door for them. "But I kind of changed my mind about Niki the Terrible. Maybe I haven't really given her a fair chance."

"What?" Alison practically shrieked. "What made you change your mind?"

Keisha looked around to make sure no one could hear her secret. "A visit to Ellie's attic," Keisha whispered. Then she beckoned for her friends to follow her upstairs to her room so that she could tell them all about her adventure in the maze.

Diary

Dear Diary,

Guess what? Niki the Terrible's visit wasn't so terrible after all. In fact, it was great. While we were baby-sitting Ashley and Ronnie, Niki had lots of ideas for activities to keep them busy. We made puppets and paper fish, and they loved hearing her play the violin. (Ronnie made her play "Twinkle, Twinkle, Little Star" at least fifteen times!) I realized that Niki isn't stuck-up like I thought, she's just very shy. And Mom told me that Niki's always wanted a little brother or sister—that's why she likes to hang out with Ashley and Ronnie so much. And you know what? They are pretty cute kids.

Boy, have I learned a lot about jumping to conclusions! Just like that security guard said, it's really important to get all the facts before you decide anything.

    I'll never forget the beautiful gardens at Longwood Estate, especially the maze. Amanda and Blair are so lucky to go to Pennington Academy—Soon Longwood will be a part of their school. When Alison heard about the maze she said it sounded so cool. Now she wants to ask our principal if we can create one on the grounds of Lincoln Elementary! (I don't want to jump to conclusions...but I have a feeling that Mr. Roberts is going to say no!)

    I'll write again soon!

Keisha